The FROGGY LIBRARY

The FROGGY
LQ
LEVINE QUERIDO
Montclair | Amsterdam | Hoboken

LIBRARY

WELCOME TO SOGGY STUMP

BY JULIE FIVEASH

COLORS BY JESS LOME

This is an Arthur A. Levine book
Published by Levine Querido

LEVINE QUERIDO

www.levinequerido.com • info@levinequerido.com

Levine Querido is distributed by Chronicle Books, LLC

Library of Congress Control Number: 2025944630

Hardcover ISBN 978-1-64614-635-2
Paperback ISBN 978-1-64614-650-5

Printed and bound in China

MIX
Paper | Supporting responsible forestry
FSC™ C008047
FSC
www.fsc.org

Published April 2026
First Printing

FOR MY GRANDMA AND CHEII

This book was written and drawn on many lands, including those belonging to the Massachusett, Potawatomi, Quechan, Cocopah, Mississauga, and Tongva people. Ahéhee' for allowing me to visit and create this book on your beautiful lands.

CHAPTER 1

So!
FROG

Anura!
What're you most excited about for this summer? It's been a quick minute since you've had this much time with Grandma!
Oh well, uh-
Hmm, looking forward to being with you of course. I haven't had a full summer since...WAY too long. And I really miss-

the gorgeous
DESERT BEAUTY!
But I don't miss how dry the air is here!
COUGH
COUGH
Drink some water, shíyázhí!
But yeah! I wanna catch up with you and Soggy Stump as a place, I feel like I've missed a lot!

Well, you're in luck kiddo!
And step one of getting re-acquainted with Soggy Stump is getting your library card for the summer. You didn't find any good books at the house, right?
Yeah...

Yesterday—
Grandma!! Do you have any books to read? I'm bored.
RUMMAGE
Yeah! I got some encyclopedias under the stairs!
Uh, hmm...
WORLD ENCYCLOPEDIA 1982 A-C
REALLY needs newer books to read

I basically live at the library back home anyway, I'll probably set up shop here too!
Ha! Well, we got a pretty cute one. I know the lady that runs it can't ever seem to sit still, so you'll have something to watch while you're there! Must be hard running the place by herself.
Do you know if they have any manga there?
What man??
Never mind...

SOGGY
STUMP
COMMUNITY
LIBRARY
STOP

Oh!
open
Cute!
Yá'át'ééh Book Lovers!
It's not a fancy library but it works just fine for us, I think!

No, I think it looks great!
I wonder if they have any good comics?
Plenty to do around here, huh? I'm sure you could find something!

Huh!
LOVE LIBRARIES?
Help is needed at the Soggy Stump Library! We're in need of part-time help with general library duties and a special project! Details can be asked at the reference desk.
So-?
Ah, well, maybe? I gotta look around the library first, get a feel for it.
I mean, I wouldn't mind having something to keep me busy this summer!

Oooh, yes, comics!
Oh, I love this movie!
Grandma, do you know if there's a limit on how many things you can check out?
Oh, this is a great suggestion!

Thanks! That was my suggestion!
Are you ready to check out?
Oh, yeah!! Let me grab my stack!
Actually, I need to get a library card first. I'm here for the summer.
WHOA
Ah, wonderful! Let me get you started with that then.
CLICK CLACK

peek
Oh, uh-
Are you all hiring by chance?
TWO WEEKS LATER-

Hey Grandma, I'm home!!
Dusty!
Oh hi shíyázhí! How's Flower's old bike working for you, lately?
Not bad!
It definitely helps with getting to work!
Flower's old bike!
- Got new tires!
- Got greased and cleaned up!
- Doesn't squeak TOO MUCH...
Ooooh, whatcha making?

Oh you know, just some-
FRYBREAD.
Wanna eat the tester?
OMG YES!
Ahem, oh yeah, I should introduce my-

QUICK FROG FACT:
FRYBREAD!
Frybread is well known within Native frog culture. It's delicious and greasy!
I personally like eating it by itself with salt sprinkled on top, but you can use it as a tortilla for a Frybread taco!
Frybread is so bad for you, and yet-

I KNOW I KNOW but it's okay to have it every once in a while. Grandma's orders!

So-
How's that new job of yours been going?
Well...
Fern is SUPER excited to have me there. I don't think they've had much help lately-
And she does pretty much everything by herself.
Help me move the books, the ceiling's leaking again!

SOGGY STUMP COMMUNITY LIBRARY
And yeah, the library is... small. BUT it's a great place to hang out. Especially if you're shy and like reading. I'm not speaking from experience!
Fern's great though, and already let me take charge of getting some new books for the "Teen Zone." I personally selected the best books I know.
Kero High School Host Club
And I think they were a hit...
TEEN ZONE

Oh and something cool happened today!
ANURA! IT'S TIME TO TALK ABOUT THE GRANT!
You mean, the grant you mentioned sorta ominously a few weeks ago when I was first hired??
It's not ominous! I was being dramatic, sheesh!
Anyway, the Amphibious Library Association has an award for libraries who want to start a community archive. I applied, hoping I'd get some money for this project, and we got it-
RETURNS
Yeah we did!!

So I hired you and now we get to start this thing! YOU mostly get to start this thing!
So we'll have money to buy storage boxes, we can finally clean what we DO have, but there isn't much of that to begin with-
Uh-
Wait-
- we might have to think about web hosting, exactly how much digitization we'll be doing (or NOT doing), and, OH, where is our scanner??
AH, OKAY FERN!
I have questions! C-could you explain the details of this project, simple stuff like what IS an archive? I have a rough idea...I think...
Oh my gosh, sorry, I got completely carried away. Let me back everything up for you.
Thank you...

An archive is more or less a collection of materials like papers-
photographs-
and recordings and more that have research and historical importance! It can reflect a community's history and people over a long period of time, if cared for!
Oh, of course!
In the past, we had an archive that was started via donations. That project was...
ARCHIVE(?)
Mismanaged by a visiting researcher. Don't get me started on that fiasco...ugh.
SO!
I wanted to build a new archive that actually reflects Soggy Stump, that gets the community members involved!

People leave Soggy Stump, leave this world, and we need to be better at capturing their knowledge while it's still around us.
I imagine this archive as a first step for the library to show its dedication to community history.
And I think it's a great first project for someone interested in library and archive work. And you said you wanted to learn more about Soggy Stump! And I would love your help while I keep the library running...
And so yeah, now I'm helping with the creation of an archive...oh boy.

I've never worked on something quite like this before but I think it's going to be really cool! Archiving itself though seems...fancy??
FERN, SOMEWHERE.
It really isn't!
Well, it sounds like a big job! And you're ready to learn what archiving is?
Yes! I had a general idea but I'm doing some in-depth research in my spare time.
Archives for Newbies!

Looking online, I keep seeing stuff on "community archives" or "community-led archives," which I think is what Fern wants.
It's the kind of archive work that's all about representing the community BY the community itself. It can be vital to local history-making and recordkeeping.
Which means this will be an AWESOME first project!
Hey Grandma, what do you think best represents Soggy Stump, like, as a community?
Soggy Stump, huh? Well, we got a lot of folks doing interesting projects.

Ooooh, like who?
close
c'mere
Like my best friend Olive.
peev
Oh, WOW, she wove that?
Olive's done a lot more than that one! She teaches weaving classes to folks in town and weaving is all she does now.
She's a busy bee with all her rugs!

Do you want me to give her a call? She could have something for your project!
Yes, absolutely!
Okay then! I'll call her right now, she should still be up watching her shows or maybe at the casino getting chile, ha!
[HEY GIRL! I got a favor to ask...YES another one, hold your horses-]
Ah, I better email Fern about this idea.
tap tap

Huh, who knew I'd find a fun way to get to know this place better? I can't wait to learn more about Soggy Stump.
Like, what makes this place my grandma's favorite? What have I been missing from Soggy Stump in all this time?

SOGGY STUMP
LIBRARY'S TOP 5
MANGA PICKS!
- CARDCAPTOR -
SALAMANDER
- KERO HIGH SCHOOL -
HOST CLUB
- CHAINSAW NEWT -
- FROGMETAL -
ALCHEMIST
- ONE POND -
CHECK THEM OUT TODAY!

CHAPTER 2

You all set for today, shíyázhí?
You're all set!
Yeah, I just put my bus card on my phone and loaded it with some money.
Wow, a card on your phone? You got the lottery numbers on this thing too?
Sorry, no can do!!
give me that...
Ah well, remember to give Olive my best, I'll be at the clinic today if you need me.
pull

Huh? Is anything wrong?
No no, just some old people stuff, should be nothing!
Also, you're going to be late, shíyázhí! You need to get going if you wanna catch that bus!
Ah, you're right! See you later Grandma!

THE HOPPER

Wow, that felt fast...
NEXT STOP- COTTONWOOD ROAD!
ARCHIVE GUIDE

Thanks!!
Gosh, I love public transit.

Huh, her house looks a lot like Grandma's.
They really are two peas in a pod.
CLICK!
Hellooooooo!

Hey kiddo!! Your grandma called ahead and said you were headed over.
OLIVE!
Grandma's friend since HIGH SCHOOL, wow!
Lives way out from town, was definitely a bit of a trip to get here!
Is an excellent weaver!
Welcome

Thanks for meeting with me today, Olive. I hope you weren't too busy!
Not at all, it's no problem! Get in here, we're letting the cold air out!
Ah, sorry! Uh, I can explain more about the project if you want but it seemed like you wanted to talk about-
OH!

Rugs
1st

EVERYWHERE

Did you make all of these??
Many of them, yes!
I've been working on rugs since I was a little froglet, helping my grandma with hers. This is a lifetime of work!
But also, anyone can start! I don't want to discourage folks who are interested in starting at age 35 or 7 or 78. Start whenever!

That's why my favorite rug is my granddaughter's first weaving, hehe.
Do you know how to weave?
Oh, uh, no, should I? Is it bad that I don't know??
CULTURAL ANXIETY!!
Oh no, learn if you want! You don't have to beat yourself up if you don't know, you learn when you're ready!
Whew, okay, I got time then.
Well, um, tell me about your classes! Grandma said you teach a lot.

Of course! I do classes all year here at my house, usually one-on-one teaching or I go into town sometimes to do a big class at the high school gym if they'll have me.
So why is teaching weaving so important to you? You could just make rugs at home and call it a day.
I could, but I feel like it would make me sad to be the only weaver! And there's so much I gotta teach.

I teach folks about how weaving was given to us by Spider Woman, the first weaver.
How weaving connects all of us and shows us how to appreciate all the things the world gives us- soil and water to grow plants. Plants to dye the wool and feed the wool givers.
And land so colorful that it inspires our designs.
I teach all these things through weaving the rug. Weaving IS storytelling. It's not always just reading words on paper.

Wow, weaving a rug can teach all of that?
Of course! Not everything can be learned from a book! Or an app! Unless...are there weaving apps?
Uh...maybe an algorithm...?
scroll...
Wait no, stop, don't actually answer that, I don't need to know! Ugh!
Just try to understand that weaving is something our ancestors gave to us to tell stories, keep warm, and pass on to our relatives.

No algorithm needed, huh? If people just look at your rugs, you think they could learn all that?
Well, maybe not ALL of that. I think folks learn best when they use their hands. Action can reinforce knowledge!
You do something enough times with your hands, it'll get into your noggin.
I know I don't learn too well when I don't have my hands occupied, ha!
rub
touch...
Oh!

Here, let me show you how to use your hands.
Yes please!

Wow, that's a LOT of work just to get a couple rows done.
Ha, I haven't even showed you where the yarn comes from!
hehe
Wait, you don't just buy the yarn from the store?
Oh, sometimes, but I mostly get it from these guys out back!
?

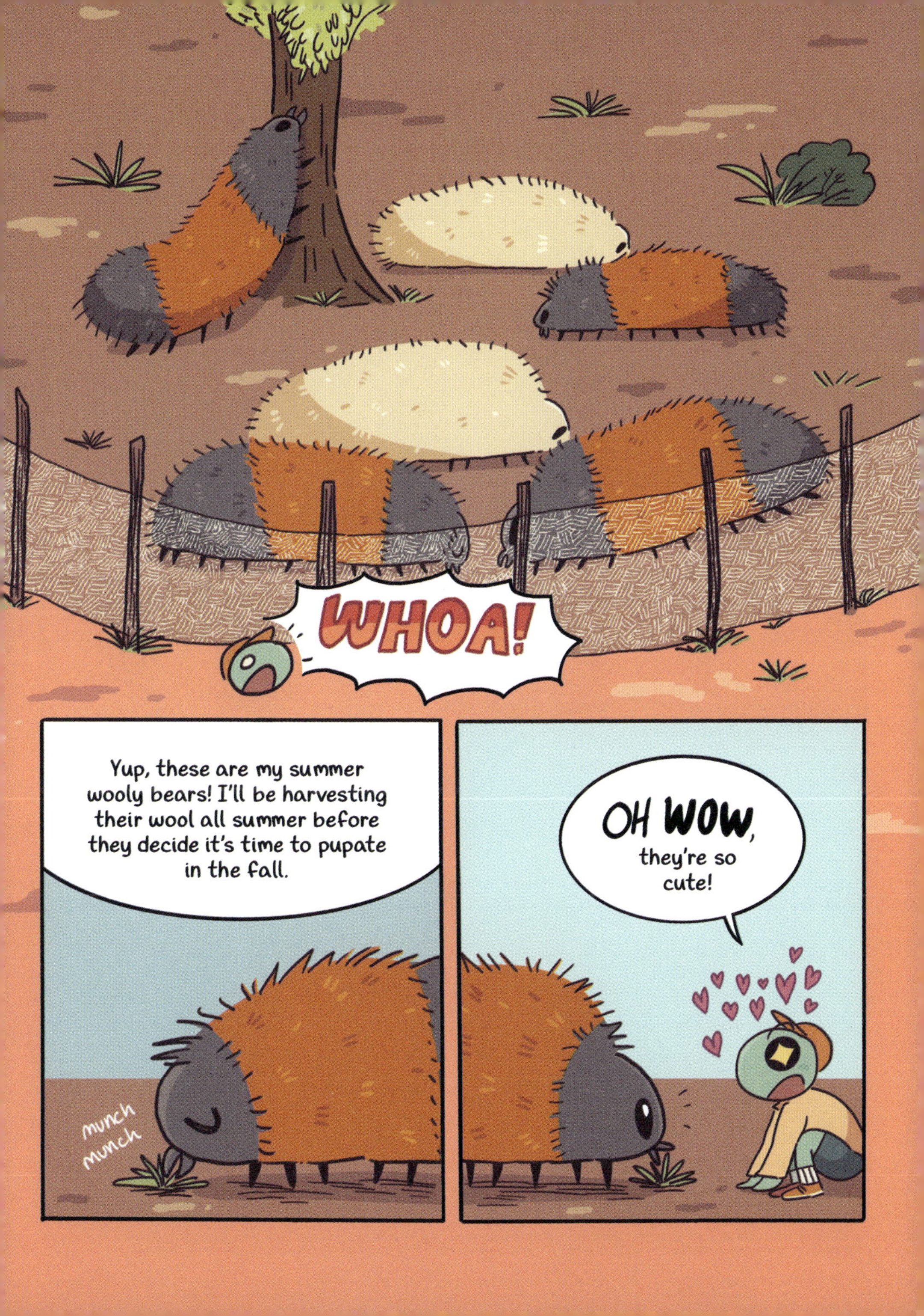
WHOA!
Yup, these are my summer wooly bears! I'll be harvesting their wool all summer before they decide it's time to pupate in the fall.
munch munch
OH WOW, they're so cute!

So the wool comes from them?
Yup! I collect it, clean it, turn it into yarn, and dye it.
pet pet
Actually, do you have some more time today? I can show you the whole yarn process if you want!
YES!
I can even show you how much they eat, HA-
Hmm...
Huh, now that I think about it, how would one archive this experience? Photos? Videos?

Would photos or videos do it justice, though?
How will folks know how much fun this is? Or how this really feels?
Making this archive will be harder than I thought...but maybe more fun than any other project I could be working on.

When it's time to shear them, do you think I could come back and help?
Of course! I always need help!
I see what you mean though about using your hands, it feels good...
It does, huh!
So keep using your hands, shíyázhí! They're some of your best tools!

Speaking of tools, I think your little archive could use some of my weaving tools, if you want! People always ask me about them and maybe folks will see them and want to know how they're used.
Oh!

Here's a few you could start with!
Wow, thank you so much- OH!

Wait, what about these?

Those are some dried plants I use for dyeing the yarn. I gotta collect a lot of them to get the colors I want.
You know what, if you want to get something else for your project, you could stop by the Soggy Stump Community Garden.
Yeah?
My friend Lavender helps run the garden and knows a LOT about plants native to around here. She helped me find some new ones to use as dye!
Oh thanks... geez...
What's wrong??

It's just that...I didn't know there was a community garden here! Or how rugs were woven. And I just feel like there's so much stuff I don't know.
Oh, dear.
Well, I wouldn't beat yourself up about that, you still have your tail, right?
Yes...?
QUICK FROG FACT!
Many frogs (not all!) start off as eggs, which develop into tadpoles-
which then develop into froglets with legs!
Our tails stay with us for a bit as we grow up, so I still have a bit of mine left!

I'm just saying, you have SO much time to learn new things, tadpole. You don't have to be in such a rush, you'll get what you need eventually.
Now, I don't want to keep you too long-
OH GOSH, what time is it??
GAH, I gotta get to the library for my shift!
Oh, and make sure to tell your grandma she still owes me a ribbon skirt!!
AHHHHH

I will!!

Later-
I'm back, Grandma!
Oh good! How was it with Olive?
Great! I learned so much about weaving! Olive even gave us some weaving tools. Fern said they'd go really well with the archive!
That's fantastic!
Do you know how to weave?
Eh, just a little. My mom knew more than me...
But I moved away for school when I got older and just never got to learn properly between kids and work. I learned how to sew well enough though.

Do you think it's ever too late to learn something like that?
Never! I'm still learning all kinds of stuff at my age. Today I learned I can look up sewing tips on my phone!
Oh, speaking of, Olive told me to tell you that you still owe her a skirt.
I know, I know, SHIYAAAAAAA that woman never lets a promise go, why'd you think I learned the phone thing!!
he he

C'mon, let's start dinner first.

NEED TECH HELP?
You've got 1 new
Need help navigating your phone, computer, or tablet?
Stop by during tech help hours, 3-5pm, Monday through Thurs

CHAPTER 3

AUTHOR
Augustine. J
TITLE
History of Weaving
DUE DATE
BORROWER

I wonder if Olive got my text...
History of Weaving
s l o w d a y
Uh...
z z z
EXCUSE ME?
OH, YES!? omg...
SLAM!

Hey, are you the one making the manga displays around the library?
MANGA IS RAD!
Yeah we said RAD! Check out the newest volumes by the Teen Zone!
Oh yeah, I mean, yes! That's me!
Cool.
. . .
Okay. Bye.

Oooookay.
BUZZ
Oh, finally!
Olive
Here's Lavender's Froggigram account for the garden!
@soggy_stump_garden
Let me know if you two hit it off! I think you're both the same age!
Thanks!!
Oh, this is cool! Look at all the plants they grow!
scroll

Oh hey, Fern? Can I ask you a question?
Of course! I'm guessing something about the archive project? You look excited!
Yes! Uh, I'm thinking of talking to the Soggy Stump Community Garden about what they do. Is that okay? I just thought they might have something interesting to add to the archive about local plants.
Ah yes, I love that idea! The garden has only been around for a few years now- they would be a great new part of the town to feature.
CLAP

Really? Awesome, I was about to message them on Froggigram.
Excellent!
Just remember to get an email from them so I can speak with them as well.
no problem!
I'm just so happy I hired you, this is going to be such a great little archive.
Stop crying, Fern! GAH!!
Anyway, keep it up!
Will do!

Okay, initiating contact!
Soggy_stump_garden
Anura_forshura
Hi! I was wondering if I could talk to Lavender? My friend Olive suggested I speak to them about the garden for my library project on community archiving. I think this garden would be a great resource for us! :)
Soggy_stump_garden
Hi! I'm Lavender! Nice to meet ya! I love Olive! What do you want to know about the garden? Also COOL LIBRARY JOB BRO
HAHA thanks!

Oh, do you mind if I also get a good email for you to introduce you to my manager at the library?
Yeah, no problem! Btw, I snooped on your profile and saw your post about Kero High, I assume you're a fan??
DO YOU READ MANGA??
• • •
Omg...
Yes!!
When I'm not knee-deep in dirt and weeds, I'm knee-deep in some high school DRAMA!!
Haha, looks like this town has more manga nerds that I thought...
text
text

The following week...
Lavender
So what else do you do at the library?
text
text
Lavender
Ahhh I saw that anime too! Did you love it?
Anura
Oh absolutely
text
text
Dinner's ready!!
Lavender
OMG did you see the terrible movie they made of Frogmetal??
Anura
YEESH, no I avoided it, haha.
text
text
text
HEY.
Huh?

Who do you keep texting on that thing? I haven't been able to get your attention in days.
Oh, just a new friend. She knows Olive and her name is Lavender, she helps run the community garden in town. I'm visiting her soon to check out the garden.
Ah...
So you've been talking about tomatoes all week then?
Oh.

Don't mind me, please keep "talking" to your new friend on your phone all day-
We're not- ugh, WE'RE JUST TALKING. This is normal friend talking! W-we're just talking about normal friend things!
Such as?
Like, uh, how she likes gardening more than schoolwork, or how she likes the same books as me, or how she's excited to meet me in person later, I dunno! She just seems really cool!
Mm-hmm...

Yes, that's all very normal and flirty, I MEAN, friendly type things to talk about.
I just think they're cool!! I don't have a ton of friends my own age here in town and she's easy to talk to! That's all!!
Okay, okay!
Do you need me to pick up some breath mints before you meet or-?
GRANDMA!!

SIGH, you're worse than Flower when I told her about this...
I'm just teasin'! Your cousin should've warned you, ha!
FROYOTA

Later-
Thank goodness Grandma's not coming today, I'd never hear the end of it from her.

Anyway, can't wait to see this garden.

Welcom
to
Soggy S
est. since

Oh!
How have I missed this place??
Hey!! Are you Anura?
Yes!
Lavender!
- She helps run the Soggy Stump Community Garden!
- Her favorite veggie is eggplant!
- She loves spending as much time as possible OUTSIDE!
Nice to meet you in real life!

Ah same! You're real! I mean, you were always real, but now you're REAL real. YUP. Really here! Um...
Great job at being-
Awkward
WELLLLLL, let me show you around!!
YES, please!
So here at the Community Garden we provide folks a space to garden and to learn about gardening.
Cool!
CLICK!

We kinda do it all over here- we usually have at least one workshop per week. We have workshops on simple gardening techniques, cooking, canning, preserving, and some craft uses.
Click!
Oh, can you explain the arts and crafts stuff you do?
Yeah! A lot of the plants around Soggy Stump can be used in a bunch of ways outside of food.
Oh, like how Olive told me about plants that are used for yarn dye. I had no idea we used so many plants for those colors!
Exactly! That's a pretty ancient use for plants!

My parents usually lead those workshops and we have guest teachers come in occasionally.
But overall, we wanted this garden to become a space where folks who move here could come and not just learn about growing plants, but what plants support us here in our town.
What do our insect friends love so much about plants? What can the trees, shrubs, and cacti tell us about this land?
All the extra veggies we grow are just a nice bonus-
CHOMP!

We do sell fruit and veggies real cheap for folks in town, or just give away what we have too much of.
Ooooh, I love your selection this week!
Wow, you totally do a lot of work around here! How tired do you get??
SO TIRED. I am completely wiped when I get home. I don't even get to read manga 'cause I fall asleep so fast!

But the work is worth it! I love getting dirty and taking care of plants and learning all there is about them. It's so much better than sitting in a classroom all day.
Oh yeah, I remember you saying something about not really liking school.
Yeah, like, I KNOW school's important, my parents are teachers after all, but does it have to all be inside?
Does learning only happen at a desk?
Yeah, if class was outside more, I think I'd be up for learning geometry or whatever way more...
Exactly!

I mean, it's kinda why we started this garden. It's for frogs who wanna be outside. For frogs who grew up here and don't always know the names of plants in their backyard.
Or the frogs who don't know how to care for a plant so that it actually blossoms or bears fruit. Folks want these skills!
We think it's vitally important to cultivate a relationship with the land, not just with folks. If you don't respect the land that grows your food and keeps you fed, what DO you respect??

Wow, she's so...*punk*.
Uh, well-
I guess I never really thought about it that way.
My parents don't really know much about plants or gardening so I never saw what I was missing.
It's okay! Honestly, creating a connection to the land takes time, and everyone finds their own path to it. Try to just appreciate what's around you first.
And you can totally come take classes here to learn that, if you want!
Oh yeah!

Anyway, enough plant talk, wanna help me pick some melons?
We can talk about the latest episode of Kero High School Host Club!
Omg, I would love that so much!

You know...

I've never really thought too hard about what the land gives us, but of course it's so much.
It's the food we eat, the clothes we wear, medicine, beauty- it's kinda incredible.
This land really takes care of us.
And if we don't care for the land, respect it, how will we all keep on living? And enjoying things like watermelon?

So-
This might be a weird or downer kind of question, so stop me if you want-
But do you ever get scared about the future?
Like, are we always going to have land and water to grow food and the things we need to live?
Sigh...no, that's a good question. I worry about the same stuff all the time.

But I gotta hope we'll be okay because it's not just us to worry about.
It's all the animals, plants, insects, and organisms that live on this land with us, that depend on all us working together in order to survive this place.
It might get harder to do so in the future, but I gotta believe we'll figure it out.
Yeah...
Okay, I take it back, that was a terribly heavy question, dude.
I'm sorry!! You had a great answer though!

I guess I'm just thinking a lot about the future and how we leave things for our future relatives to remember us.
Making an archive brings a lot of this up. Like, will photos of what we're doing right now even be enough to remember us years in the future?
That's certainly a tall order for your project. I hope it can capture the little details too- like the smell of this watermelon.
Ha, well I'll try my best!
Oh, speaking of future relatives, I just had an idea!

Welcome to my "office!"
Office
Wow, your office kinda smells.
Scratch that, your office absolutely *reeks.*
My office used to hold most of the manure for the garden, you know, like any well-stocked business office.

Some of these...and these... oh definitely those-
Some tiny future relatives for the archive!
Oh, SEEDS! *HECK YES!*
And I'll get you some instructions for all of these. Folks can help the future if they know how to grow these babies!
White Sonora
Palo verde
Kaña
Yes! I gotta looking into making a *seed library* of some kind now...
snap!
Ah, it's getting late. Think I'll have to start heading home.
Okayyyyy...

But thanks again for stopping by. I had a great time!
You'll have to come back so you can borrow my original *Frogmetal Alchemist* DVDs!
Wahhh, YES. Also, feel free to stop by the library with them. Fern would totally love to meet you!
And be sure to come check out books and the archive when it's all ready!!
I wouldn't miss it!!

Also! Anura! Try not to get too bummed out about the future! You can always do something about it!
Everything will be okay if we try to make it be!
Listen to your friends! Things will be okay in the future.

Everything will be okay...

The next day...
POND AREA!
Please leave NO mess!
Hmm...feels slightly too warm...
Splash!

QUICK FROG FACT: PONDS!

Frogs need constant sources of water, so Soggy Stump has plenty of public ponds around.

It's a great way to cool down and necessary for new parents and tadpoles.

They also make great meditation spaces!

How was the community garden? And Lavender??
Great! I got some seeds for the archive and even got an awesome idea for a seed library we could install here!
Oh that's such a great idea! There's always some project I wished I had more time to work on and a seed library is exactly one I've been wanting to do! Anura, you're totally fulfilling my goals for the library!
I think I'm creating all new goals for myself! Between the seed library idea and the archive, I've got my work cut out for me this summer!

Well, before we get ahead of ourselves with more projects, let's make sure the archive is in good shape!
Have you been working on the finding aid like I asked you last week?
Yes! I'm not done at all, but I'm working on it bit by bit!

Oh, and before I forget why I came out here in the first place, could you help me clean up around the manga shelves?
Those emo teens really wrecked the place today. They even left a bunch of tiny comics everywhere.
Tiny comics??

I ALMOST regret convincing those emo teens to gather here...
I guess it's good they're reading at least.
"Tiny comics"?
OH!
"Soggy Comix"....?
Thanks for reading.
Printed at Soggy Comix

TADPOLE READING HOUR!
Every Tuesday and Thursday at the Library Pond! 10 - 11am!
Come get your kids into reading!

A TEA INTERMISSION...

OMG Flower!! I'm so excited to try this tea flavor at Tadpole Boba, you gotta come here the next time you're in town!
NEW!!
TRY OUR NEW— FLY HIBISCUS TEA!
Yes! Oh, and the shop is really cute!
ORDER HERE
Please place your order here!
Ooooooh, touchscreen ordering! I know, fancy for Soggy Stump!
Okay, I'll call you later! Have fun at camp!!

Now what did Grandma want...?
Ah yes, the grandma flavor. **Blaghhhhhh...**
Butterscotch Fly Eggs
- An oldie but a GOODY!
NOW WITH MORE BOBA!!
...
One hibiscus tea!
That's mine!

Gotta wait for Grandma's tea- oh WAIT. I recognize that frog.
They came up to me the other day at the library...should I say hi...?
HEYYYYYY- it's me from the library! The frog at the circulation desk?

H-how are you liking One Pond? I see you're on volume 30.
ONE POND
Oh, huh, yeah it's okay.
~ SILENCE ~
Soooooo, do you like the library?

Yeah...it's cool...I guess...
And...??
I mean, it's cool you're adding lots of manga and comics to the book selection. Makes it worth going to the library.
OH! WOW, thanks!

But, uh, I have other ideas about the library, if you care at all about bringing in more weirdos like me...
ONE POND
Oh, "weirdos" is a strong word but I'd love to hear more about your ideas!
Oh yeah? Well, uh, chill for a bit if you want...
Oh, what's your name by the way??
...Sage...

The next day-
Fern!!! Sage here wants to work at the library!!
I said I'd *THINK* about it or whatever...
End of break!

CHAPTER 4

One dragonfly donut for Anura!
Yes, right here!
Dang, these are SOOOO good...

heh-
okay...
Set
Go left in 200 feet!
So I didn't spend that much money this month, so I should be okay to buy some books today at-

GET YOUR COMIX!!
HOURS
MON - 11-6pm
TUES - 11-5pm
WEDS - 10-7pm
THURS - 11-6pm
FRI - 11-7pm
SAT & SUN - 11-6pm

GET THE LATEST ISSUE OF WOGMEN!

BOOK SIGNING!!
HOURS
COMIX
The comic shop...WOW...

Okay...
OPEN!
Don't go nuts and get distracted. Remember, you work at a library, you technically have all the books you need! TECHNICALLY!!
Oh, gotta text Grandma.

Made it to the comic shop! Are you at the casino with Olive?
...
PING!
?
Oh!
Ha!
LOL, have fun you two! See you at dinner!
Have fun too honey!!
Okay, don't get distracted by all the books, don't get distracted-

Welcome to Soggy Comix!
THIS WEEK'S COM
oh, WOW.

MANGA
HEROES
indie
OMG
OMG omg
omg
omg
OMG omg
OMG
omg

45 minutes later...
OH SHOOT! I got distracted! GAH!
POP!
POP!
POP!
LOCAL COMICS!
INES!
Can't get any comics in front of me, I swear-
LOCAL COMICS!
ZINES! ZINES!
HEY WAIT!

These are the ones I found at work! There's even more of them!
5 BEST EMO BANDS ACCORDING TO ME
heart BREAK, now...
ZINES! ZINES!
And they WERE printed here!
"Zines?"
THESE ZINES WERE PRINTED HERE AT SOGGY COMIX! ASK AT THE COUNTER ABOUT PRINTING YOUR DEBUT ZINE!
Ahem!
I see you're perusing our awesome self-published shelf!
Yes!

Are you interested in making your own??
Yes! WAIT, no! WAIT, not no, but not right now! I'm here to ask a question or several!
Haha, sure thing!
OMICS!
Is this a "zine"? What is a zine? Is it a comic? Something else??
Also am I saying that right? "Zeen"? Or is it z-AYE-n??

Well, let's start with the word: it's said like zEEn, like magazine!
Secondly, it CAN be a comic, but it could also be poetry, photography, whatever you want to print!
Think of them as self-made, printed pamphlets. You fill them with whatever you have to say and then give them out!
one page zine!
perfect bound zine! (fancy!)
hand sewn binding
half page zine!
spiral bound zine!
accordion zine!
mini
zines!

WHOA, and you can make those here?
Yeah! But we mostly sell comics and graphic novels here (with some other stuff as well).
I see you already got a couple of books picked out for yourself!
hello!
Not looking at those right now!!
Anyways, we understand how hard it is to get published and you gotta start somewhere! So the store tries to encourage self-publishing by offering it here. The first 20 copies are on us!
Be nice to me!!

Oh, so do you teach how to make the zines?
Oh no no no, I love comics and I appreciate the heck out of them but can only sell them. No artistic talent over here!
Luckily, I got amazing staff members who can do stuff like that, like Gemma over there!
Wow, well you probably get this question a lot but...why do you like comics and zines so much?
Why run a store devoted to them? Why not run a regular bookstore?
My young friend, that question never gets old for me!

what the heck?!
this is COOL...
I, Moss, owner of Soggy Comix, have loved comics since a small child. They helped me learn how to read and they gave me a love of reading!
Comics gave me hope- they inspired me by combining words and art in such a way that made stories come alive right from the page! I was hooked!

GRAND OPENING!
Welcome!
I opened this shop when I was just out of my froglet years, when I wasn't sure what I even wanted to do! I hoped it would turn out okay...
I hoped it would give me a purpose, but twenty years later it's given me a family, a community- it became more than I ever thought!

Also, it's never boring! One of the best parts of this job is being able to provide so many types of comics: kids comics, how-to comics, superhero of course. You can find a comic for nearly anything! Stories and knowledge, for me, are just better as a comic!
I agree! And this all re-affirms everything I thought about comics! I mean, is there anything they can't do??
Well, comics are sometimes *just* comics. We get plenty of folks who come in and want to argue about the "best" *Uncanny Frogmen*... those folks won't *ever* go away...
will you STOP!?
Are you NUTS?!

But comics cater to many different readers! Folks learning how to read-
For folks trying to learn a new language-
Or just something new! They're a great educational tool!
He...ran... up...the...
What was that character again...?
COMICS TO COOK TO!
Omg, exactly! I know what you mean!
I learned to read REALLY early as a tadpole, thanks to comics!
Mom! Come turn the page!
They're still the number one book I get from the library!
Yes, you get it!!

In short though, we just love comics around here. Everyone should read them, young and old. And everyone should try making them! If you do, we can keep them on the shelves!
F
Ah, sorry for the old toad ramble! You got me going!
Oh no, not a problem at all. You got me thinking that maybe I should sit down and make my own comics and zines...
Well-
If you want to try that, Gemma here can show you some steps!

SO you wanna make comics and zines, huh??
UH-
Yes? I mean, I did until you got real serious about it there, but I think I still want to-
EXCELLENT!
Sorry, I swear I'm normal about this, BUT FOLLOW ME!
Okay, we're going to start off with the easiest zine to make.
Grab that piece of paper and let's go over some-

QUICK ~~FROG~~ ZINE FACTS!!
Zines have been around for nearly a century, starting off with the sci-fi fanzine! Zines are sold or traded by creators called, "zinesters" and at events called, "zinefests!"
Zines are basically the coolest ways to make a little book of your choosing.
Today we're making the "one-page zine." This starts with a 8.5" x 11" sheet of paper, aka regular letter-sized printer paper.
1
Next, fold that into eight equal sections and then unfold.
2
Next, fold it in half, hamburger style!
3
And then, using scissors, cut from the folded middle to the middle of the folded half.
4

Your paper should look like this when unfolded now. Your last steps will be to fold it together!
5
Now, after you've cut it, keep the middle parts sticking up and then take each side and pull them away from each other.
6
7
When it looks like a four pointed star, you're nearly there!
Fold the paper inwards until it makes a little book.
Then fill it with whatever you want- you made a zine!

OH MY GOODNESS, it IS a little book! That's WAY too cool!!
Oh wait, so how do I make more copies of this thing?
Great question! You'll use what you just made! And a scanner!
So, since this is on letter paper, you can scan and copy this on a regular office scanner or copier to make more copies!
The original zine you drew on is called your "master copy."
Be nice to me!!
And feel free to make an orientation guide to remember which way the art/writing should go!
1
5
6
BACK COVER
FRONT COVER

Wow, I can see why so many of the teens at the library are obsessed with making these!
Poetry
They're super easy to make and fun to fill with your thoughts and art! I'm always happy when folks stop by to make them!
omg this is so sick...
Gah, that's so cool! You all have the coolest jobs at the comic shop!
Heh, we totally do.
Oh, here, I'll leave you some supplies to let you fill in your zine.
Thanks!
ZINE SUPPL

10 minutes later-
Omg, why is this so hard, I've drawn before but this feels like I have to get it just right...
No, just draw, it's your first attempt at a comic! Nothing is ever perfect! It won't get made unless you DO IT. THAT'S how you pep talk!!
poke poke
I'm definitely not AMAZING at drawing but...that bike looks all right?
UGH, just keep going! No one's going to look at the bike that hard!!

Okay, I'm sorry, this is pretty bad and I need to learn how to draw better and-
FIVE BEST PLACES TO
OMG!
Ahhhhh, I knew it was bad!!
No no, stop, it's *PERFECT.* AH, I didn't even know about some of these spots. You did a great job drawing and describing them!
This is what zines can do! You helped me learn something new about the place I live!

But I-
Nope, stop doubting your abilities to use art to teach someone something!
Ugh, you're so right.
GASP, I could make a zine about everything I just learned about weaving. And gardening. I could have Olive or Lavender help me!
Oh, do you want to sell your zine at the store?
Later-
FIVE BEST PLACES TO
NEW!
Wow...
Who knew becoming a published author was THIS EASY?

What a cool place to just talk about stories all day...

THE SPIRAL
GEMMA'S REC!
Well-
I think I gotta get going but I wanted to thank you again, Gemma. For showing me the zine stuff!
Oh, no problem!
Seriously, come back any time and we can make more zines!
Also, don't be discouraged about your art! It all takes practice.
I won't! There's too many cool things I wanna talk about now!
But I really need to learn how to draw bikes...

Moss, thanks again for showing me around the store. I didn't get to mention it earlier but I'm buying these zines to add to a new community archive at the library.
Really! That sounds great! If you want, let us know if you ever want to collab on a comic workshop or author reading, we'd be happy to work with the library in town.
BOOP!
Of course! I'll definitely tell my manager, she'll love that idea!
Oh and are you purchasing these?
Riiiiiiiight...
Hello again...

One slightly painful purchase later-
I was SO good today, I only got THREE books I could've totally gotten from the library.
Soggy Comix!
And geez, I have so many ideas for zines now thanks to these. They'll also look so cool in the archive!
desert
poetry
FIRST AID TIPS!!
Who would've thought frogs were publishing their own work here in Soggy Stump!
Soggy Comix!
I should tell- *OH!*

Oh dang, I put my phone on silent. 20 missed calls??
20 missed Calls!!
Hello?
What.

Anura,
it's your grandma.

CHAPTER 5

A few weeks ago...
Grandma?
Is it "fun" getting old?
Or like scary? Or both??
Ha! Both I think. I dunno, getting older can have its moments from time to time.

I think I'm excited to get old, be someone with a big bushy beard.
Who tells lots of stories to all my little relatives...
Cheii mode
Gotta get some stories to tell first...
What are they rambling about now??
Ah, you'll get those stories one day. Don't be in such a hurry!
Getting old can definitely be scary, I suppose.
Your body starts to creak, you don't move as well any more but... it's worth it to watch your young relatives grow into themselves and learn more about yourself too.
The learning never stops, really.

Like this app you showed me the other day!
I can learn all the Bunaza trivia I could ever want on this thing!
Grandma, you've seen every Bunaza episode at least 50 times, how much could you NOT know at this point??
Well, I gotta live long enough to find out, huh?
That's fair! Wahhh, my food!
Haha!
ha, ah-
cough

COUGH cough cough
Are you okay?
I'm okay, but uh-
Need me to grab your inhaler?
COUGH If you could shíyázhí.
COUGH!
cough!
cough...

A few weeks later.
SOGGY
STUMP
COMMUNITY
LIBRARY

Grandma...
Pull
Look at how big you are now!
I'm SOOOO big now!
Grandma, I missed you soooo much! Way more than FLOWER.
I dunno about that-
HEY!

Grandma-
Oh, here's one of when Cheii wasn't a Cheii yet!
Grandma-
Yá'át'ééh, I'm over here!
Grandma-
Ahahaha
Oh shush she didn't say that-

Grandma?
COUGH COUGH COUGH
GRANDMA!
EMERGENCY SERVICES
Olive, how's Grandma?
swallow

A-C
D-F
Um?

??
Huh, what, what was that?
I said, are you okay, Anura?
No.
W-what? Yes, YEAH, I'm fine-
WIPE

No, they've been staring at that shelf and not moving for like 10 minutes. It's been like this all day.
They're totally out of it.
Thank you for your honesty, Sage. Please go ahead and work in nonfiction for now.
Anura, I'm sorry again about your Grandma, but I want you to know you don't have to be here.

I know I don't need to be here but I...I don't want to go home either...
I-I'm sorry! I shouldn't be here like this-
No, no, it's okay.
You worked so hard to be here: building our new archive, expanding the collection-
Heck, just that brought in Sage.
Sit
You've done good work but you can't hide behind it right now.
The library will still be here if you take a break!

But I haven't finished the community archive. I can't just leave it-
As your manager-
I'm telling you to leave it! Those materials will be right here!
I'm sorry if I pushed the project too hard on you, but I'm asking you know to take a break before...well...
You need to take time for your grandma and for yourself.
Don't worry about any of this, just take a deep breath for me-
ha-
And then let it all out.

Okay okay, you're right! I'm taking a break starting now!
Thank you, Anura, and please, take your time!
But uh, before you head out-
I love Sage, we all love Sage, Sage is totally the best.
BUT, could you tell him to redo the kid's shelf? Books are supposed to be stacked *vertically* along the shelf, not in *piles*...
Saaaaaaage, don't make me regret this recommendation already!
CHILDREN'S BOOKS!
Hmm, a new shelving system??

Fern is right though, I should be with Grandma as much as possible right now.
Work wasn't as great of a distraction as I hoped...
We're going to try and stay upbeat about-
Grandma having to be in hospice.

HEY ANURA!
HEY!
VEGGIE SALE TODAY!
STOP

Hey you!
Do, uh, you need an eggplant by any chance?
Thank you so much but no, I'm good, thanks!
I'm totally good...
Um, how are you feeling?? With everything I mean.
I know it's a lot, but are you taking care of yourself?
Not feeling amazing! Attempting to keep calm about this all.
I was actually on my way to see her at the hospice.
...how is she?
Uh, comfy, I think?
That's what it looks like anyway... when I see her...

. . .
So...how's your family doing?
Oh, uh-
My parents came over already and the rest of them are all slowly coming into town, at least the ones not already here.
I'll tell them to stop by the garden!
They can't possibly miss this eggplant, it's probably the best eggplant around!!
HAHA, okay!

But seriously, thanks for checking up on me lately. I know I haven't watched all those videos you've sent me...
7:15
You have 25 messages from
No, it's fine. I sent those hoping you'd watch them as a pick-me-up. Never feel obligated to watch them all!
It's just, you know, my way of saying I'm thinking of you.
sending the third funny tadpole video of the day
Thanks again for that...
I-
C-can I actually give you a hug?
OMG, get in here!!

Thanks...
Don't forget I'm here, okay?
I won't, I promise.
You're not alone...
VEGGIE SALE

But that doesn't mean this isn't hard.

SOGGY STUMP HOSPICE
Yeah, yeah, I'm okay, I'm doing fine.
It's actually super beautiful today.
Oh wow, yeah.

Oh hey, I'll call you back, my nerdy cousin just got here.
HEY!
Hey you!
QUICK ~~FROG~~ FLOWER FACT!
Flower is Anura's cousin on their mother's side, they share Grandma Juniper!
Flower is good at, like, EVERY sport ever, dang!
Flower secretly loves reading just as much as sports but she won't admit it...
Go away!!
2

I'm so glad you're here Flower...
Back at ya. Here, let's sit.
It really is nice today.
Yeah.
So...Grandma's not...getting better is she...

No, she's not. The asthma attack left her without oxygen too long and it's...not good.
We're just waiting it out until... yeah...
Oh, you know what? I don't think I can go back to her house.
Oh, why?
Everything there just screams "GRANDMA," you know?
Our photos are all over the walls, our height measurements, the smells, so many memories are hard-baked into it...it all makes me so sad.

Yeah, it's hard being there now, but my parents and I gotta water her plants and keep the place nice in the meantime...
You know-
Sometimes I wish I was a tadpole again so I wouldn't have to remember how awful I feel during this.
?
You don't have to worry about a thing if you only have one thought at a time!
You say that...
And still, I've been collecting memories all summer for work.
The archive shouldn't have *these* kinds of memories in it...it's not fun!

Well, not every memory is going to be fun. I'm sure your archive can't prioritize only fun memories, right?
Yeah, you're right. It's not really reflecting the community at large if we just skipped all the hard parts.
What kind of community archive would that be...
Speaking of-
Do you ever feel like... you didn't listen to Grandma enough?

Like, you knew the things she was trying to tell you were important but-
You just didn't always have time to stop and listen before you had something else to do...
Or-or you thought you'd have more time?
And how it's like all of those stories and conversations are falling through your hands before you have time to catch them?

Yeah...
If-
If I could remember anything right now, in this time that we still have her-
It'd be this sky, I guess.
Oh!

SOGGY STUMP HOSPICE
CLICK

Okay, well, I'm going to head out and get some food. Do you want anything?
No, I think I'm good.
I'm just going to sit with her for a while. Feel free to join us later.
STAND
Okay, just remember to text me or my mom if you need anything.
Of course.

Okay...
SWOOSH
Go make memories with her, good OR bad...
breathe

BUNANZAAA!!
Hey, her show is on-
Beep
Beep
And she's missing it.

The doctors said it all happened too fast...we just have to make sure she's comfortable now...I hope she is.
She was driving me around town just a few weeks ago and now...
Hey-
Little Joe's just a boy, go easy on him, y'hear?

He doesn't know any better, give him time.
The summer wasn't supposed to be like this.
This-this isn't fair.
Sniff
I didn't get enough time with her...
FWHUP
I didn't learn enough from her-
Sniff
I didn't-

I don't have enough time.

There's always too much...I'm running out of room in here.
rummage
And there's never enough time to hear everything...
RADIO MIX #7
This pack is getting harder to pick up by myself.
But I gotta get moving if I wanna outrun the storm.

I'm so tired and hungry, but there's still so much stuff to collect and archive and I-
GRanma's FRY BREAD!!
Just around the dead stump!→
Oh, frybread...
Okay, I can take a **quick** break!

GRANMA'S FRYBREAD!!
Made it...
Oh heyyyyyy, shíyázhí, come on over!
I'll get a fresh piece ready for you.
turn turn
Put that big pack down, it looks heavy.
Oh, you're right, it totally is...

Grandma-
SODA
Do you have any memories I could collect?
I've been picking up as much as I can around here, but-
FWISSS
Ohhhh, so *that's* what's in your pack?
I've got a lot more in the back if you wanna check!
Bread will be done in a second!
SLIP

Oh-oh no...
This is way too much..I..uh...

And the storm's still coming towards here...
Bread's ready!
Grandma, it's too much.
I only made you one piece of frybread-
No no, everything back there.
I-I can't collect all of those memories.

Oh that back there?
Well, of course, that's too much for anyone to collect.
I'm old though, our memories build up like that.
But don't worry about it!
The storm will come and wash it all away.
But I don't WANT IT TO!
How will I learn about your life?
Our history??
I never learned how to properly make frybread like you-

I didn't learn the language, I don't know any of the prayers or songs like you do- I-I don't know anything!!
And it's all going to be washed away when you-
W-when you d-
PLIP!
Ah-

No, I-
Shíyázhí, come here.
Oh Anura, my Anura...

Grandchild, all of that back there, it'll get swept away because I'm going soon.
The next world is waiting for me-
So that's why I need to collect it! Let me grab something, anything- I really don't know enough!
I can't learn without you!
I know it seems like you have to do this with me, but even when I'm gone, our history, our language, it'll all still be there for you.
You still have family and friends on this world who will teach you once the storm passes- it can't stop that.
You're never alone in your learning journey.

But...it would be easier with you...
I know...but I need to get ready for what comes next, shíyázhí.
And you, you need to look at what you've already collected.
You mean this stuff??
No, no-
I mean *these!*

These are your real archives.

But...that's just stuff I did.
They're not books or recordings or notes-
Yes, but-

They don't need to be those things in order to be an archive.
Food is an archive, these plants, this dirt, that mountain-all an archive.

All of these beings hold a record of us, of themselves, and we aren't tied to pieces of paper.
Our stories, our spirits, our knowledge can't only be contained to a box.
I'm not just my box of old aprons, right?
N-no-
No, you're the smell of breakfast in the morning.
You're big, deep hugs after a long absence.
You're stories late at night when everyone else has fallen asleep except for you and me.

Hold onto those and let the storm come.
It'll wash my body away, but never those memories. You're going to discover so much in your life, even without me.
I love you, my child.

CHAPTER 6

So-
TADPOLE'S FIRST SWIM!

I keep having this *other* dream that I'm in my grandma's house...
And she's there.
But she's taking down all the framed photos in her hallway.
And she's saying-
We're getting new photos pretty soon, so we won't need these anymore, huh shíyázhí?

And I say-
It's okay to leave a couple of them up!
How else will I remember your face?
And she looks like she's about to laugh real hard-
But then I wake up.

And then I wake up.
Sorry if that's a bit sad! Just trying to recount it all.
No no, never, it's okay! I'm just glad you're texting again.
Yeah, it's been a rough few months but it'll be nice going out to visit her.
I bet!! Tell her I said hi!
And I hope she approves of the flowers!! I chose only the best blooms!
Oh I'm sure she will, don't worry!

Ah I'm at my stop already! Sorry, talk to you later!
AH!
Talk laterrrrr!
Desert Lawns
HOURS

Oh!
Olive!
Oh, Anura!
It's so nice to see you! How's it going, shíyázhí?
It's fine!

I see you grew some hair out! It looks good!
Yeah, I needed a little bit of a change, I guess.
I- uh, picked these up from my friend.
Oh, they're lovely.
Thanks...

You know...
We're not really supposed to come back to where someone is buried...
but it was such a nice day today.
JUNIPER
BELOVED GRANDMA, MOTHER, SISTER, AUNTY

I just had to come tell her about it.
Ah, I get it.
And show her how good I look in the skirt she made!
I feel so lucky she was able to finish it before... *sigh*...

Well...
It turned out great!
Good job Grandma!
Worth the wait?
Worth the wait!
I came today because I wanted to bring her the flowers and-
I, uh, *attempted* to make these this morning with my mom. They're...well you'll see...

Definitely too dark
Weeeeiiiiiird shape
100% made with love
Awww, Anura, she'll love that.
A good first try!
JUNIPER
Frybread isn't exactly ancestral food though.
If you want, you can always come by my house and learn some new recipes.
Oh Olive, that would be awesome!
I need to try making something that won't burn the kitchen down.
Haha, sure thing!

BEEP BEEP BEEP!
Ah, that's my alarm, I gotta run to work!
I'll see you in a little bit!
Quit running on frog time, shíyázhí!!
Oh, that kid.

Later-
Where's that other table...?

Hey-
So you spent a lot of time on that archive project, right?
Yeah, a good bit of time.
Then please tell me how setting up tables and chairs is "archive work"?
Isn't it supposed to be working with papers and boxes and stuff?
uh...

Well, yes, the archive work is collecting the materials-
describing the materials-
putting them in boxes and folders, and it's good and all-
But it's boring as heck.
It *can* be kinda boring as heck (not always though).
And-

While I did all those steps, it ultimately felt like something was missing.
Yeah?
So much of Soggy Stump felt, to me at least, like it was tied to action?
And that action was being done with other people? And everyone's knowledge that was being added to the archive didn't feel like it was capturing all of that.
I looked at the boxes of what we collected and didn't understand how it could tell a community story without the action being present, to reinforce the knowledge.
So, I talked to Fern and we agreed that...
maybe archive work could look like this!

Weaving Workshop Today!
Join us at 3pm!
. . .
Or...not??
Hey, what's up Sage?
I just...well...

I see this library that's kinda small.
Oh sorry, lemme just-uh- get past you there, SORRY!
And kinda falling apart-
Ugh, not again...
Wet Floor
And I wonder... does anyone actually care about what we're doing?
. . .
My dad didn't care that I got this job.
And when does anyone stop by and say, "WOW good job, you all!" Rather than, "OMG libraries are still a THING? WHO KNEW?!"

I think that's a bit harsh-
So what, you make an archive and then... what??
Folks **suddenly** realize how deeply important libraries are??
They just give us more money and resources out of the blue and fix everything broken here?
out of order

Be real, nobody cares about this archive!
Just like how nobody cares about this library!
And nobody cares about this town!!
I CARE!
And...my grandma cared.

And Fern cares!
And actually, YOU CARE.
You always act like you're SO over this whole place but you come into work anyway!
You're helping me today with an event and a gathering you don't even think will work!
Because you WANT it to work!
Because you DO care!

And so what if we're the only ones who care about the library and archive right now?
We're not going to stop trying to make events happen. Or stop trying to give patrons a reason to come in and start to care!
THIS MONTH'S LIBRARY EVENTS
Maybe others only care a little bit right now, but that care can build up over time, after the fifth, sixth time they stop by to learn something.
I have a book to pick up, Fern!!
I can't promise we'll make things better in a day, Sage. Or with just one collection.

But I'm sorry it's hard for you to see why this all matters right now.
I can't expect you to see the future or anything but you gotta trust me that down the line...
You'll want to have been there to learn these things when the chance was there. While the people who come and share these stories are still around...
sniff sniff
You miss your grandma pretty bad, huh.
Every dang day, dude.

Sigh...
Look, I was totally being harsh.
And that wasn't cool of me.
I get hot-headed sometimes, whatever.
But it wasn't fair when you've been so chill with me.
Especially when you're... yeah...
Also, I'm sorry I snapped at you earlier.
It's okay, I get it.

...
Okay, get in before someone sees.
Ah, are you sure??
I wasn't sure you EVER gave hugs...
YES OMG, STOP STALLING.
Holy moly, it's-
FRIENDSHIP!
WHOAAAA

This feels...like I'm only going to get this once. Once in a *lifetime.*
Yeah, I mean, basically. I don't just give hugs out, enjoy it.
You gotta stop being such a downer, Sage.
Absolutely not.
READING IS RAD!!
FREE WI-FI!
pat pat
Weaving Workshop Today!
Join us at 3pm!

Soon-
HEY KIDDO, SLOW DOWN!
Heyyyyy, Lavender? Right?
Yes! Nice to see you again!
Hello! I'm Moss, local business owner! First-time weaver!
Is that so?

Gah, I can't believe this is happening!
Oh, it's happening!
And then again next month! I hope we get another good turnout!
'Cause you never know with these events...
Uh, Fern?
This...isn't all for nothing, right Fern?

Have you been talking to Sage?
I mean yes, but he sort of had a point- what if no one cares about this work?
What if this all goes nowhere?
Well, do you see anyone here who doesn't seem to care about this event?
Huh...

Not at all.
Well, that's probably your answer then.
Just keep doing what you're doing, Anura. It'll come together eventually.

Sage-
C'monnnn!
Ughhhhhhhh...
Fine, I'll go say hi, ONE TIME.

Hey guys, meet Sage!
Hiiii Sage!!

Is this the weaving workshop??
Yes!

The End!
SOGGY STUMP
LIBRARY CARD

Ahéhee' for reading!

Oh my goodness, thank you so much for reading all of that! I'm truly, super duper happy that I completed my first book! And that you got to read it! WOW! I can't say I always knew what I was doing while making this but hey, that's the creative process for ya. Here's to the next one being even better!

I could not have finished this book without the awesome support of my editor Nick, my fabulous book designer Andy, and my amazing colorist Jess who really brought this book to new heights. Another big shoutout to my friends Rusteen and Damon for looking over my thumbnails and giving me much-needed feedback. And to my wonderful partner, Tom, for supporting me with tea and snacks while I finished this thing. My cats, Pepperjack and Cheddar, get no thanks as they were extremely unhelpful but loving distractions.

This book would also not exist without the ongoing work of librarians but specifically tribal librarians, who are doing vital knowledge and information work for their respective communities. This book was always for them and for those who now fight so hard to keep their libraries and archives open despite every effort to close them down for good. Knowledge is sacred, easily taken away or lost, and our Indigenous knowledge keepers know this better than anyone. Please do whatever you can to support tribal libraries now and for future generations to come.

And now, for some extras...

The Cast

Anura

Character traits: Bright, anxious, excited, worried

Favorite food: Frybread taco

Fun fact: Anura's name comes from the scientific order name for Frogs!

Grandma Juniper

Character traits: Gregarious, unstoppable, loud laugher

Favorite food: Caterpiller stew

Fun fact: Grandma Juniper is in spirit named after my real life Grandma June!

Olive

Character traits: Patient, hardworking, big teacher-vibes

Favorite Food: Blue corn mush

Fun fact: When she's not weaving, she's watching her shows like *Days of Our Amphibious Lives.*

Fern

Character traits: Optimistic, stressed, possibly over-worked...

Favorite food: Strawberry sundaes

Fun fact: Fern is the youngest library manager ever at Soggy Stump Community Library!

Lavender

Character traits: tough, hard-working, outdoorsy

Favorite food: Anything that can be made using garden veggies

Fun fact: She's convinced that if she ever got a desk job, the sitting alone would seriously harm her.

Sage

Character traits: Done, over it, doesn't care

Favorite food: Green Chile burritos

Fun fact: Sage was already looking into working at the library when Anura met him but took it as a sign to apply once Anura got involved.

Flower

Character traits: Active, outgoing, sporty

Favorite food: Fried fly skewers

Fun fact: Flower is loosely based on my real life sporty cousins!

Moss

Character traits: Talkative, lively, caring

Favorite food: Green chile pizza

Fun fact: Moss writes a monthly column about selling comics that's fairly popular in the comic-selling frog sphere.

Gemma

Character traits: Pumped, always ready, excitable

Favorite food: Bagels

Fun fact: When she's not dealing out comic recs, she's planning new art for the shop's window display!

Some more about Soggy Stump

While Soggy Stump isn't a real place, it's based on the very real places I grew up in, Arizona and New Mexico!

Much of the houses in Soggy Stump were based on housing you would find on the Navajo rez and in places like Tucson. I grew up in small desert towns so I drew a lot of inspiration from that kind of setting.

Soggy Stump is just one small town in this froggy world that I'm crafting. There will be more places to explore in future stories but this story takes place in the desert region of a larger land that's similar to ours.

The very first iteration of what would become Anura was this "adventure frog" I made way back in 2020!

I liked the overall look of Anura when I started designing the book but GAH, they didn't have clothes!!

While I liked the bandana, it wasn't necessary going forward when I started giving them clothes to wear.

Bonus Comics!

So are they...?

The Hat

Sarah

And they were...

A Very Short Diné/Navajo Word Glossary

Ahéhee' (*uh hyeh heh*): Thanks!

Cheii (*chey*): Maternal grandfather. Also said as shicheii, or my grandfather. We have words like this because Navajos have a clan system which we use when greeting each other. You would list your your first clan, which is your maternal grandmother's clan, which comes from her mother and her mother's mother and so on. The second is your paternal grandmother's clan, so your dad's mom. The third is your maternal grandfather's clan, and lastly your fourth clan, your paternal grandfather's clan.

Diné (*Deh nEH*): The people! Specifically the Navajo people, it's our way of referring to ourselves. Diné and Navajo are both used pretty interchangeably these days when talking about ourselves.

Shiyaaa: Basically SHEESH but in Navajo, ha!

Shíyázhí (*She ya zhee*): Basically son or little one. I thought it would be a cute term that Anura would be called by their grandma.

Yá'át'ééh (*Ya aT ehh*): Hello or greetings, or very literally "it is good."

Thank you to Navajo Word of the Day (Navajowotd.com) for always having great mini lessons on words!

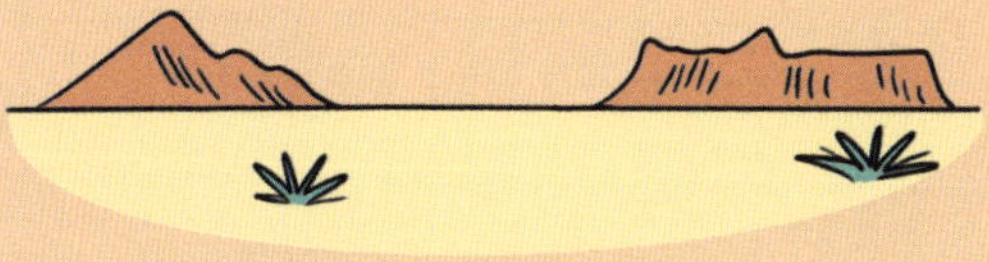

JULIE FIVEASH (they/them) is Kinyaa'áanii, born for Naakai. Their maternal grandfather's clan is Táchii'nii and their paternal grandfather is Bilagaana. They are a nonbinary Diné cartoonist and zinester, stationary fiend, and former Librarian for American Indigenous Studies at Harvard University. Based in Los Angeles, they were raised in Yuma, AZ. You can find them at @jooliefiveash.

The Froggy Library is their debut.

JESS LOME is an illustrator and colorist based in the Midwest. She graduated from a small community college and has been doing art professionally ever since. She currently has 4 cats who all "help" her with work (totally don't just sleep on her keyboard).

SOME NOTES ON THIS BOOK'S PRODUCTION

Art for the book was done by Julie Fiveash using Procreate on their trusty iPad and brushes from Wendy Xu. With drawing inspiration from countless volumes of manga checked out from the Los Angeles Public Library and rug design inspiration from *Spider Woman's Children* by Lynda Teller Pete and Barbara Teller Ornelas. Colors were done by Jess Lome, using a large XP-Pen screen drawing tablet and Photoshop. The text was set by Fiveash in Pretzel by Sara Linsley; the display type was hand-lettered. The book was printed on FSCTM-certified 120gsm Golden Sun uncoated paper and bound in China.

Production supervisor: Freesia Blizard

Managing editor: Danielle Maldonado

Designer: Andrea Miller

Editor: Nick Thomas

LQ